LifeRich Publishing is a registered trademark of The Reader's Digest Association, Inc.

LifeRich Publishing books may be ordered through booksellers or by contacting:

LifeRich Publishing
1663 Liberty Drive
Bloomington, IN 47403
www.liferichpublishing.com
1 (888) 238-8637

ISBN: 978-1-4897-2150-1 (sc)
ISBN: 978-1-4897-2151-8 (hc)
ISBN: 978-1-4897-2152-5 (e)

Print information available on the last page.

LifeRich Publishing rev. date: 02/07/2019

This book is dedicated to my
four delightful grandchildren

Mary, Will, Matthew and Timothy

MARY SUE'S

Kooky Diary

by Maureen B Caffrey

Illustrated by Izzy Bean

Mary Sue, a child of eight,
Went to sleep each night
very, very late!

She gobbled some candy
tucked away in her sheet
And had kooky dreams that
kept her from sleep!

Her Grandma told Mary, "Write
your dreams in this book.
That way other kids
may have a look.

'Cause everyone has dreams,
as I'm sure you know.
Write them down, Mary
Sue. Just give it a go!"

So Mary Sue, a child of eight,
Took pen in hand at night
really, really late!

She thought about one kooky night
When her mom came in
to turn off the light.

When she tiptoed out
and said good night,
Mary Sue grabbed some
candy and took a big bite.

She tossed and turned and
just couldn't sleep.
The house was quiet, and
there wasn't a peep.

When finally Mary Sue
fell off to sleep.
What appeared in her room
was a giant white sheep!

She hopped out of bed
to give him a hug
But flew in to the air when
she slipped on her rug!

A giant sheep tried to
catch her midair.
But it was too late, for
she fell on a bear!

A bear got in, but she
did not know how.
Then she spun around, and
there stood a cow!

How did these big creatures
get into her room?
They were flying all around,
zoom, zoom, zoom!

She shouted out loud,
"Mommy, Daddy, come see!
There are animals everywhere
looking at me!"

So her parents rushed
quickly to Mary Sue's bed
Just as she yelled out,
"Those animals fled!"

"It was only a dream, Mary
Sue," her Mom said.
"Get under your covers,
and stay in your bed!"

The very next day Mary
Sue woke in fear.
"Did I really see a bear
and fall on its ear?"

"No," said her mom. "It
was only a dream.
But Daddy and I heard
you let out a scream.

No more candy for you
just before bed.
It puts silly ideas in your
sweet little head."

But Mary Sue, a child of eight,
Still gobbled her candy
and stayed up late.

So she wrote in her diary
each and every night
About all those kooky dreams
that gave her a fright.

Mary Sue has nightmares
and wild stories to share,
So, kids, read her next book,
that's if you dare!

CPSIA information can be obtained
at www.ICGtesting.com
Printed in the USA
BVHW091407040319
541707BV00015B/593/P

9 781489 721501